we don't eat our CLASSMATES

HEY, KIDS!
You will never be
eaten by a T. rex.
They are extinct.
I promise!

NEW YORK TIMES BEST-SELLING AUTHOR
RYAN T. HIGGINS

Disney • HYPERION
Los Angeles   New York

To Mom, for passing along her love of books
And to Dad, for making me a storyteller

I would like to thank Ava B., Ava H., Cecilia, Cora, Delila, Eben, Griffin, Jillian, Kaden, Karen, Kelsey, Lexie, Luna, Noah, Penelope, Quint, Sam, Theodore & Willow for their help with drawing dinosaurs.

First Edition, June 2018
20 19 18 17 16 15 14 13
FAC-039745-21284
Printed in South Korea

This book is set in Macarons/Fontspring
Illustrations were created using scans of treated clayboard for textures, graphite, ink, and Photoshop
Designed by Phil Caminiti

Library of Congress Cataloging-in-Publication Data

Names: Higgins, Ryan T., author, illustrator.
Title: We don't eat our classmates! / by Ryan T. Higgins.
Other titles: We do not eat our classmates
Description: First edition. • Los Angeles ; New York : Disney-Hyperion, 2018.
Summary: When the class pet bites the finger of Penelope, a
tyrannosaurus rex, she finally understands why she should not eat her
classmates, no matter how tasty they are.
Identifiers: LCCN 2017036131• ISBN 9781368003551 (hardcover) • ISBN 1368003559 (hardcover)
Subjects: • CYAC: Tyrannosaurus rex—Fiction. • Dinosaurs—Fiction. • First
day of school—Fiction. • Schools—Fiction. • Humorous stories.
Classification: LCC PZ7.H534962 We 2018 • DDC [E]—dc23
LC record available at https://lccn.loc.gov/2017036131

Reinforced binding
Visit www.DisneyBooks.com

 Penelope Rex was nervous.
 It's not every day a
little T. rex starts school.

"What are my classmates going to be like?
Will they be nice?
How many teeth will they have?"

This was very important.

Penelope's mom bought her a new backpack
with ponies on it.

Ponies were Penelope's favorite.
Because ponies are delicious.

Penelope's dad packed her a lunch of three hundred tuna sandwiches

and one apple juice.

Finally, the big day came,

and Penelope Rex was very surprised to find out that all of her classmates were . . .

So she ate them.

Because children are delicious.

"Penelope Rex!" said Mrs. Noodleman,

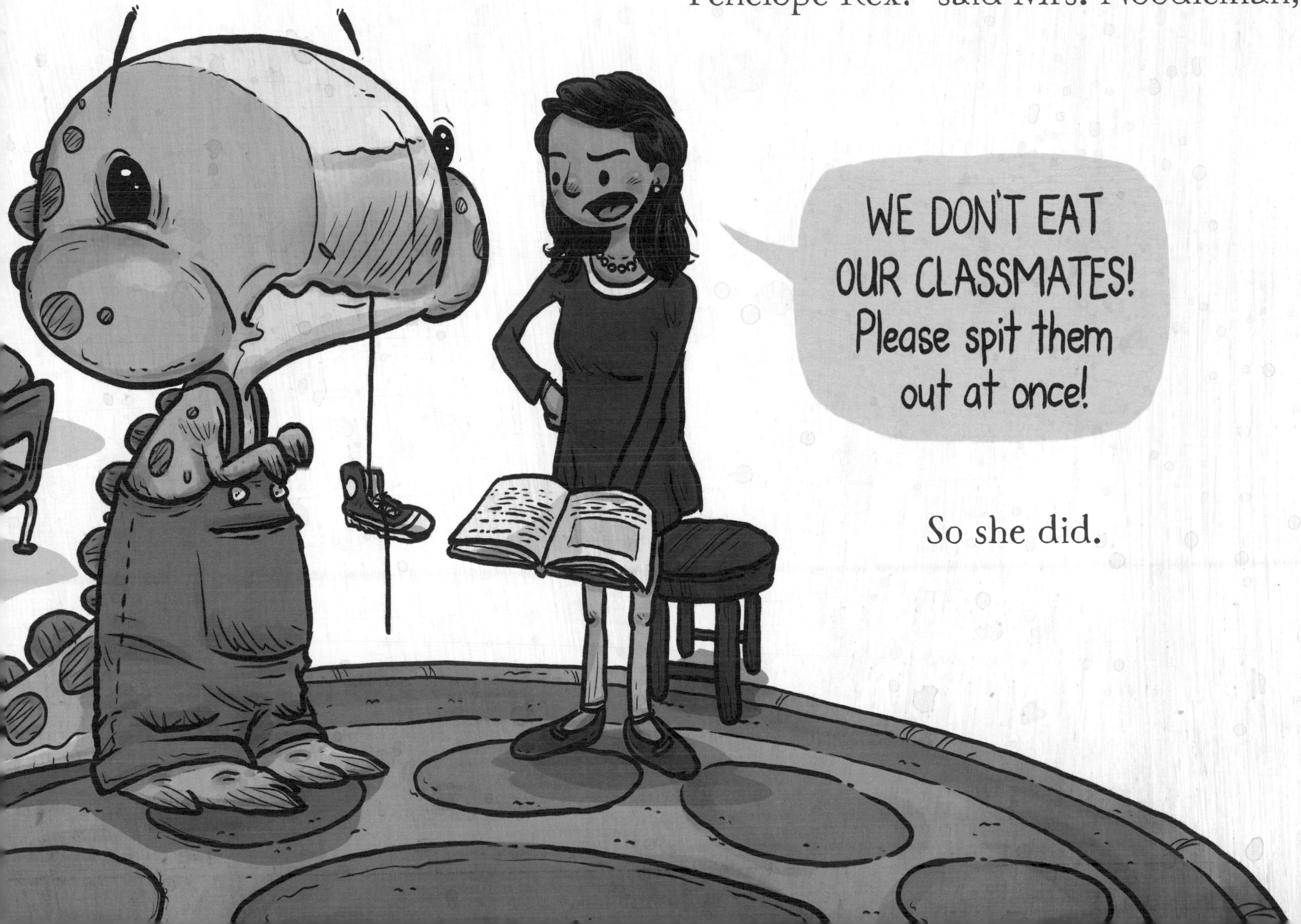

So she did.

It was NOT the best way to start school.
Still, Penelope was determined to have a good first day.

She tried hard to make friends at recess.

She finger-painted some of her best work.

Penelope started to notice everyone was making friends but her.

It was lonely.

When she got home, her dad asked about her first day of school.

"I didn't make any friends!" Penelope cried. "None of the children wanted to play with me!"

"Penelope Rex," her father asked, "did you eat your classmates?"

"Well . . . maybe sort of just a little bit."

"Sometimes it's hard to make friends," said her dad.
"Especially if you eat them."

"You see, Penelope, children are the same as us on the inside. Just tastier."

That gave
Penelope
a LOT to
think about.

The next day Penelope
tried REALLY hard!

But poor Penelope.
She could not stop herself
from eating her classmates.

Mrs. Noodleman,
Penelope ate
William Omoto again!

And they were all afraid of her.

Except Walter. . . . Walter was a goldfish.

So Penelope tried to
make friends with him.

Will YOU
be my friend?

"EEEEEEEEEEEEEEEEEE!"

cried Penelope.

"He's eating my finger!"
"WAAAAHHHHH!"

Once Penelope found out what it was like to be someone's snack, she lost her appetite for children.

She stopped eating her classmates. . . .

(Even when Cece Woodman
spilled BBQ sauce
all over herself.)

And soon Penelope made friends!

Now, even when children look especially delicious,
she peeks at Walter and remembers what it's like
when someone tries to eat you.

And Walter, the goldfish, stares right back at her and licks his lips.

Because dinosaurs are delicious.